TE

ROBOT?

For teachers everywhere
(especially the human ones!) - DC

To Phoebe and Cameron - CE

STRIPES PUBLISHING LIMITED
An imprint of the Little Tiger Group
1 Coda Studios, 189 Munster Road,
London SW6 6AW

A paperback original
First published in Great Britain in 2020

ISBN: 978-1-78895-067-1

IS MY TEACHER A ROBOT?

ILLUSTRATED BY

DAVE COUSINS   CATALINA ECHEVERRI

CHAPTER 1

ON THE LAST DAY
OF CHRISTMAS

"A ROBOT?" Dad snorted at the TV.
"That's just a vacuum cleaner with a face
painted on it!"

We were watching the *Buy It or Bin It?*
Christmas special. People go on the show and
present an invention to a panel of investors.
The panel then decides if the idea is worth an
investment and buy it, or reject it to the bin!
Mum and Dad were hooked.

"Fleur looks quite interested," said Mum, as
the camera zoomed in on one of the judges.

"She lived round here, you know," said Dad.

"You say that every time," I told him, rolling my eyes.

Dad shrugged. "She's worth billions!"

The woman on the telly was called Fleur Pickles. She was probably about the same age as Dad, but she looked … less worn, somehow. Being a billionaire probably helped. It was good to know that somebody from a nowhere town like ours could get rich and even end up on TV.

"We should get Grandma to go on this," said Dad. "The stuff she invents is way better!"

Mum nearly spat out her chocolate. "Are you serious? Have you forgotten what happened when Digby got too close to that **AUTOMATIC TURKEY STUFFER** she made? The poor dog hasn't been the same since!" She shuddered. "And as for that **SNOW MACHINE** … we're lucky it was only *our* windows that got broken. Those hailstones were the size of golf balls!"

"Yeah, but think of the money she'd make if she sold one of her ideas," said Dad. "Where *is* Digby, anyway?"

"With Robin, I expect."

Robin is probably Grandma's most successful invention. She built him to look after me and Jess while Mum and Dad were at work. He looks so much like a real person, most people don't even realize he's a robot.

The judges on *Buy It or Bin It?* were about

to announce their decision when we heard an ominous crash from the direction of the kitchen.

"I'll go!" I said quickly. Mum and Dad quite like having a robot around, but Robin has a habit of getting into trouble. They got rid of him once before – I didn't want them to have a reason to do it again.

I made sure to close the door behind me.

"Is that YOU making all that noise?" My sister was standing at the bottom of the stairs, scowling. It's her favourite facial expression. "Have you seen Digby?"

"I think he's in there … with Robin." I nodded towards the kitchen.

"So what are you waiting for?" Jess is always telling me what to do – like she's my *big* sister, when in fact we're twins, so exactly the same age.

"Why don't *you* go in?" I said.

"You're closest!"

I sighed and opened the door.

The kitchen was unrecognizable. It felt as though we were walking into a jungle made from Christmas paper, dangling like multi-coloured vines from the ceiling.

I was barely over the threshold when something lurched at me from the undergrowth. It was like a giant spider, all spindly limbs and quick, jerky movements. One of its arms ended with a pair of shining blades that snipped the air in front of my face.

I ducked, narrowly avoiding an unscheduled haircut, then stumbled into a transparent web of sticky tape.

The creature pounced.

In seconds I was wrapped in a Christmas cocoon, unable to move.

"Robin!" I shouted. "It's ME!"

"Master Jake! Oh, my!" The robot apologized and started to cut me free. "You stepped into my production line. I thought you were a gift that needed wrapping!"

"You do know Christmas is over, right?" said Jess.

"But your mother was disappointed when your grandma's **RAPID-WRAP-IT!** machine didn't work," said the robot. "I thought I would see if I could improve on it."

"I don't think Mum wanted you to gift wrap the kitchen though," I said.

Robin stroked his beard, a sign
he was thinking. "My procedure is still
in the development stage. I repeat a task
and refine the process until it runs smoothly."

"It's a good job you've got a whole year until
next Christmas," said Jess. "I'd say *this* process
needs a *lot* of refining!"

I looked around at the web of tape
stretching across the kitchen, bits of wrapping
caught up in it like festive flies. "By the way, have
you seen Digby? I thought he was with you."

"Digby? He's just…" Robin turned towards
the pile of presents. "Oh dear!"

We'd rescued Digby and were trying to *unwrap* the kitchen when the doorbell rang.

Dad's footsteps thumped along the hall, then we heard our neighbour's voice.

Mr Burton reminds me of a vampire. He has a pointy nose and grey bushy eyebrows like two hairy caterpillars clinging to his forehead.

We watched through a crack in the door as he handed Dad a note. "It's a bill," he said. "For the damage your robot caused to my house when it malfunctioned."

Me and Jess exchanged a look. We knew a lot more about Robin's *malfunction* than anybody realized – but that's another story.

"This seems expensive!" said Dad.

"Removing chocolate muffin from a cream carpet is not easy," said Mr Burton. "Besides, there was the leaf-blower." He shuddered.

Even I'd been surprised how powerful *that* had turned out to be.

"I must go and apologize," said Robin. "Your father should not have to pay for damage I caused."

"NO! Don't go out there!" I put my body between Robin and the door. "It's better if Mr Burton doesn't know you're here."

Meanwhile, Dad and the old man were still talking.

"There may be an alternative solution," said Mr Burton. "If the robot was to come and work for me, he could repair the damage himself – at no cost to you."

"That proposal is a very logical solution," said Robin. "I wish to accept."

"NO!" said Jess. "Have you forgotten what happened last time?"

"Mr Burton treated you like a slave!" I reminded him. "He made you cut his toenails!"

But the robot wasn't listening. He made
another lunge towards the door, so Jess jumped
on his back while Digby took hold of a trouser
leg in his teeth. But Robin is surprisingly strong,
and even the three of us together couldn't stop
him.

Dad looked surprised when the kitchen
door flew open and Robin burst into the
hallway with me, Jess and Digby still clinging on.

"I wondered where you lot were," he said.

"Where's Mr Burton?" said Jess.

"He left." Dad raised an eyebrow. "I'm guessing you were listening?"

"You're not going to make Robin go and work for him are you?" I said.

"I told him I needed to talk it over with your mum."

"It is right that I should repair the damage I caused," said Robin.

"Well … hopefully it won't come to that." Dad smiled. "Now, I don't suppose there are any mince pies left, are there?" He moved towards the kitchen but Jess jumped in the way.

"I'll get you one! Why don't you go and sit down? You don't want to miss the end of *Buy It or Bin It?* do you?"

Dad nodded. "Good point! Thanks, love!"

"That was close," said Jess when he'd gone. "Jake, you help Robin clear up this mess while

I keep Mum and Dad distracted with mince pies."

Normally I would have argued, but I was too busy thinking that Mr Burton would be back, and it was going to take a lot more than mince pies to keep *him* distracted.

WHY DOESN'T HE
JUST LET GO?

"What's *Happy New Year* in Russian?" said Ali.

This was my best friend's favourite walking-to-school game. He liked to ask Robin random questions such as, "How many bananas would it take to reach the moon?" Answer: one point nine billion. Or ridiculous maths puzzles like, "What is the square root of the sum of 5,334,426 divided by 592,714?" Answer: three!

Ali and Jess's friend Ivana are almost the only people outside of our family who know that Robin is a robot. Grandma said we had to keep it a secret in case bad people found out what Robin could do and tried to steal him for their evil schemes.

The robot stroked his beard while he processed Ali's latest question. "*S novym godom*," he replied, in a deep Russian accent.

"It's similar in Croatian," said Ivana. "*Sretna Nova godina!*"

"I wish my brain had a direct link to the internet so I could know everything," said Ali. "I'd be a boy genius!"

"No, you'd just be a boy with direct access to the internet," said Jess. "You'd still be an idiot!"

"Yeah, but I'd get all the answers right at school!"

"You could try listening in class," my sister pointed out.

"That's *hard*!" said Ali. "Robin can just download information. I only have to tell him something once and he knows it forever. My mum says she reminds me of the same things every day and I still forget. I try to remember but the stuff just won't stay in my brain."

"Probably because it's so small," said Jess. "Not enough room."

But Ali wasn't listening. "Whose car is THAT?" He pointed at a huge black vehicle with tinted windows parked in the *NO PARKING* zone outside the school gates.

We were still gawping when the back door swung open and Olivia Sharpe stepped on to the pavement.

My sister groaned. "Who else would it be?" Olivia is Mr Burton's granddaughter. She and Jess aren't exactly best friends.

"Is that a … DOG?" Ivana pointed at the ball of white fluff Olivia was holding.

With its pink ribbon and glittery collar the dog looked sweet enough, but the moment it saw Digby, the creature erupted into frantic, high-pitched barking. The next thing we knew, it had jumped out of Olivia's arms and was hurtling towards us.

Robin was holding Digby's lead, so when the dog fled into the school car park, the robot went with him.

We watched as Digby dodged between two parked cars then leaped over a low wall – Olivia's dog snapping at his tail. Robin followed, clinging on like a terrified water-skier as the dogs zigzagged through a line of trees and then dragged him through a holly bush.

There was a gate at the far side of the car park. It was locked, but the bars were wide enough for a small dog to squeeze through.

Sadly, they were NOT wide enough for a person … or a robot.

But Robin is loyal. Digby is his friend. No way was he going to let go of that lead.

"Let's sit him down in one of the comfy chairs," said the school caretaker, helping us carry Robin into the staffroom. "I really think we should call an ambulance."

"NO!" I didn't mean to shout, but if paramedics examined Robin they'd find out he wasn't human! "He'll be fine. He just needs a moment."

But Robin didn't look fine.

"He's probably got concussion," said Ali, when the caretaker finally left us alone.

"Do robots get that?"

Ali shrugged. "How many fingers can you see?" he asked, holding up three fingers.

Robin blinked, but didn't answer.

"Maybe his voice processor got damaged?" said Ali.

Grandma had given Robin an upgrade over

Christmas. She'd swapped his roller skates for black shoes with wheels hidden inside, found him a new stylish wig, and replaced his speech processor with one salvaged from a car satnav system. It was more advanced than his old one, so maybe there was more to go wrong?

"You could try switching him off and on again," said Ali. "That's what I do when my computer goes funny."

"Might work." I checked there was nobody watching.

"WHAT ARE YOU DOING?" said Ali, as I pushed my finger up Robin's nostril.

"The reset button's up his nose. Grandma put it there so it couldn't get knocked accidentally."

"Gross!"

I held the button until Robin's body went limp. Then I pressed it a second time, praying he would start up again. If the caretaker came back now he'd think Robin had died!

I was relieved when I heard the muffled whirr of fans as the robot restarted.

Then the bell rang.

Ali jumped up. "We need to get to class!"

"But Robin's not ready yet! It takes him five minutes to reboot."

"Can't we leave him here and come back at break? We'll be late!" Ali is terrified of getting into trouble. "Nobody's going to come in. All the teachers will be in class."

"I suppose…" I didn't want to get into trouble either, especially not on the first day back.

We joined Jess and Ivana at the back of the line waiting to go into the classroom.

"We caught Digby and left him with Mr Binder in the office," said Jess. "How's Robin?"

"He was acting a bit weird, so we had to do a reset." I stabbed the air with my finger.

Jess winced. "But he's OK now?"

"Yeah, should be."

My sister's eyes narrowed. "Well, is he or isn't he?"

"I don't know, do I? He was still rebooting when the bell went."

"You mean you LEFT HIM?!"

"He'll be fine," I said. "As soon as he wakes up he'll get Digby and go home."

"I knew I shouldn't have left you two looking after him. You had ONE job!" My sister shook her head. "If anything happens to Robin, it's YOUR fault!"

THE TERRIFYING TALE
OF IGGY PIGGY

I was so busy thinking about Robin that I
didn't notice who called us into class. With
all the drama, I'd forgotten that our teacher
Mrs Badoe was away having a baby. I looked
up and saw Ms Sternwood standing in the
doorway. This was BAD! It's not that our head
teacher is particularly strict, the problem is
HER GUITAR! Ms Sternwood thinks that
turning everything into a SONG makes
learning more fun. She has songs for fractions,
geography and science. She even has a song

about our class pet, Ham the hamster!

And then … there's 'IGGY PIGGY'.

When you're in Reception or Year Two, it's just a funny song about a pig. Not so much when you're in Year Five and Ms Sternwood is making you perform the song **IN FRONT OF THE WHOLE SCHOOL and PARENTS** at Sharing Assembly. Especially if you've been chosen to play the title role, which means you have to stand up at the end of every chorus and say, **"OINK! OINK!"**

"Don't worry," said Ali. "She probably won't make you be Piggy again."

But as we took our seats I saw the guitar leaning against the teacher's desk.

"I have some lovely news," said Ms Sternwood. "Mrs Badoe gave birth to a beautiful baby girl on Christmas morning!"

"Was it born in a stable, miss?" It was difficult to tell if Brett was joking. Sometimes it was difficult to tell if Brett was even awake. He saved his energy for picking on people during break. (Mr Burton is *his* grandad, too, so you can see where Brett gets it from.)

Ms Sternwood frowned. "Er ... no, Brett. She was born in hospital."

Brett looked disappointed.

Jess raised her hand. "Are you going to be our teacher now, miss?"

"I contacted the agency to arrange a substitute," said Ms Sternwood. "They promised to send somebody as soon as they can, but until then I'll be taking over."

She smiled. "How about we start the new term with a sing-song? Hands up if you remember the words to 'Iggy Piggy'!"

But before Ms Sternwood could pick up her guitar, the school secretary appeared at the door. "Sorry to interrupt," said Mr Binder. "Your substitute teacher has arrived."

"Oh!" said Ms Sternwood. "How lovely." But you could see the disappointment on her face. "Read quietly until I'm back," she told us.

"Wonder who we'll get?" said Ali, as the head teacher left the room. "I hope it's not that Mr Mitchell!"

"Which one was he again?"

"Grumpy old guy with a beard. Made us sit in silence and had a go at Sanjit for breathing too loudly!"

"Oh, yeah, I remember."

"We might get Miss Bonnet!" My friend blushed as he said it.

Miss Bonnet (pronounced *Bon-ay*) was young and French, and Ali had acted very strangely during the week she'd covered for Mrs Badoe.

"Here they come," said Ali, opening his book, not noticing it was upside down.

But the person who followed Ms Sternwood back into the classroom wasn't young and French.

He wasn't old and grumpy either.

But he did have a beard...

I felt my jaw drop.

Ali's book slid to the floor. Standing next to the head teacher with a slightly dazed look on his face ... was Robin. "This is Mr Mitchell," said Ms Sternwood, indicating the robot. "He's going to be your teacher this term."

All I could think was that the school secretary must have found Robin in the staffroom and assumed he was the substitute teacher. I noticed that Ms Sternwood's glasses were still on the chain around her neck (she never remembered to put them on). To the head teacher, Robin must have looked like Mr Mitchell, the bearded substitute teacher. But why hadn't the robot explained who he really was?

"Maybe he's forgotten who he is?" whispered Ali. "The accident might have scrambled his circuits!"

I nodded. If the accident *had* messed up Robin's memory … perhaps when Ms Sternwood and Mr Binder assumed he was Mr Mitchell, the robot believed them!

I watched the figure standing at the front of the classroom. He *looked* like Robin, but at the same time … different somehow. I tried to catch his eye, looking for a sign that he knew who I was, or perhaps more importantly – who HE was! But there was nothing.

Somebody had recognized him though.

Olivia's hand was waving in the air. She and Brett were the only other people in school who knew Robin was a robot.

Ms Sternwood looked up. "Yes, Olivia?"

"Miss, I just thought you should know that's not—"

28

The end of her sentence was drowned out by a loud crash from the back of the room.

"Sorry!" said Sanjit. "Fell off my chair!"

Olivia's moment was ruined.

Ms Sternwood shook her head. "I think I'll leave Year Six in your capable hands, Mr Mitchell."

Olivia's hand was still waving furiously. **"MS STERNWOOD!"** she shouted. **"THAT'S NOT MR—"**

But the head teacher had gone.

I WILL TEACH AND
YOU WILL LEARN

Robin watched Ms Sternwood leave then
turned to face us.

"Good morning, class," he said. "My name is
Mr Mitchell."

"No, it's not!" said Olivia. "You're Jess and
Jake's babysitter!"

There were a few gasps of surprise and
everyone turned to look at me and Jess.
After his Christmas makeover, it didn't surprise
me that nobody else realized that *Mr Mitchell*
was actually the weird roller-skating guy in the

old-lady coat who used to meet us from school. But then, neither did the robot apparently.

"I'm afraid you are mistaken," said Robin. "I am Mr Mitchell. I have no connection with anyone called *JessandJakes* and I most certainly do *not* sit on babies."

Half the class burst into laughter. It was hard to tell if they were laughing *at* Robin, or if they thought he'd deliberately made a joke.

"I am a teacher," he said. "The role of a teacher is to deliver education." Robin must have looked up *How to be a teacher* online. Unfortunately, it made him sound much more like a robot than a teacher. "You are my students," he said, pointing at us. "I will teach and you will learn."

"If he keeps talking like that, someone's going to guess he's a you-know-what!" Ali muttered.

Grandma had preprogrammed hundreds of key phrases that Robin could use when he met people on the school run or in shops — things to say that would make him sound more human. Sadly, she hadn't prepared *a set of useful phrases you'll need should you find yourself teaching Year Six on a Monday morning.*

A collective gasp from the class made me look up.

Robin had written *My Favourite Thing* on the whiteboard.

"Wow!" said Ali. "Does he always write that fast?"

I'd forgotten that Robin could do things at super robot speed!

Ivana put up her hand, which was strange because she's normally too shy to speak in class.

"What education do you require, Student Ivana?" said Robin.

A rash of giggling broke out across the room.

"Pišite sporije ili će pretpostaviti da niste čovjek!" said Ivana.

"What did she say?" Ali whispered.

I shrugged, but the next time Robin wrote on the board, he did it at human speed.

"She must have told him to slow down!" I said. "She did it in Croatian so nobody else would understand!"

My best friend gave Ivana a look of pure adoration. (For some reason Ali thinks Ivana is great – don't ask me why.)

But Ali wasn't the only one who was impressed. All around the room hands were shooting into the air wanting to know if Mr Mitchell was from Croatia like Ivana's family.

"No, I am fluent in a number of languages," said Robin.

Sanjit raised his hand and said something in Hindi and the robot replied. Suddenly, anyone in the class who could speak a different language was trying it out on Robin.

Gradually, the whispers stopped being about how WEIRD Mr Mitchell was, and we heard people saying he was kind of cool.

Then Clara raised her hand. She sits in the front row because she has difficulty hearing. Mrs Badoe used to wear a special microphone around her neck to help Clara hear what she was saying. When the robot pointed to her, Clara used sign language to ask her question. Barely pausing to stroke his beard, the robot signed a reply.

For a moment I thought the class was going to break out into a round of applause. Then Robin told us to get out our exercise books and write about our favourite thing, signing simultaneously as he spoke.

"Maybe this is going to be OK." Ali unzipped his pencil case. "I always thought Robin would make a great teacher."

"Yeah, but that's not really Robin!"

Ali shrugged. "Would you rather be singing 'Iggy Piggy' with Ms Sternwood?"

"No, but…" I wanted Robin back. He was part of our family. I didn't need a robot for a teacher!

When Robin told us we had five minutes left until break, I'd barely written two sentences. I was supposed to be writing about how gaming was my favourite thing, but I was too worried about Robin to concentrate. Then I had an idea. I wrote about how my babysitter Robin had helped me and Ali complete the final level of our favourite game. I wrote how great he was – that *he* was actually my favourite thing. I hoped that when Robin read what I'd written, it might trigger a memory and bring him back.

CHAPTER 5

DESPERATE TIMES CALL FOR DESPERATE MEASURES

When everyone else piled out into the playground at break, me and Ali hung back.

Robin was reading through our writing books at lightning speed.

"Have you read mine yet?" I asked.

"Yes," he said. "The Robin person sounds very skilled at his job."

"That's YOU!" I told him. "You're Robin – my babysitter!"

The robot shook his head. "I am Mr Mitchell, your teacher."

"But—"

He pointed to the playground. "You should join your classmates outside. Fresh air and exercise stimulates the brain. It will help you receive education when you return." Then he turned back to the books.

"Maybe we should try another reset?" I whispered.

"You mean stick your finger up his nose again?"

"It might put him back to how he was."

Ali frowned. "But what if it does something else? We didn't expect him to turn into a teacher. What if we reset him and this time he decides he's a KILLER ROBOT or something?"

I stared at him.

"Anyway," said Ali, "if we get Robin back it means we won't have Mr Mitchell, which means…" He nodded towards the guitar still leaning against the desk.

Before I could reply the door burst open, and something small and hairy hurtled into the classroom followed by Jess and Ivana.

"DIGBY!" said Ali, rushing to greet him.

But there was only one person the dog wanted to see.

The robot jumped to his feet. "Get that dog out of here!"

Digby skidded to a halt and sank to the ground, his eyes filled with confusion. He looked up at Robin and his tail gave a hopeful twitch.

"It's Digby!" I told the robot. "He's our hairy little brother – remember? He's your best friend!"

Robin looked at the dog and stroked his beard. He HAD to remember him!

"There *is* a saying among humans that a dog is a man's best friend," said the robot. "However, I am a teacher. I do not tolerate dogs in my classroom. Please remove it immediately."

I looked at the others. I could see that they were thinking the same as me: if the robot didn't even recognize Digby, Robin was truly gone.

The classroom was in semi-darkness when we got back after break.

"Are we going to watch a film, sir?" said Sanjit.

Robin nodded.

"Oh, no!" I grabbed Ali's arm. "You remember when you came round ours to watch the new Spider-Man movie?"

"That was so cool!" said Ali. "The way Robin

beamed the video from his eyes on to the …
oh!"

"Exactly!" I said.

"If he does that here everyone's going to
know he's not human!"

"EXACTLY!"

"I enjoyed reading about your favourite
things," the robot was saying. "Thirty-six per
cent of the class wrote about pop singer and
actress Carly-G."

Olivia and her friends grinned at each other.

"Last week Carly-G was in New Zealand
recording a promotional film for her latest
song, 'Baby Baby Baby'," said Robin. "I am now
going to educate you using this video."

"What are we going to do?" said Ali. "He's
going shine 'Baby Baby Baby' from his eyes! IN
FRONT OF EVERYONE!"

"Desperate times call for desperate
measures," I said. "Hit me!"

"What?"

"Punch me on the arm! If we pretend to have a fight, Robin will come over to break us up. Then we can tell him not to use his video eyes!"

"But we'll get into trouble!"

"Desperate times, Ali!" I said. "I'm sorry…"

"Sorry, for wh— OW!"

"I thought you two were best friends!" said Mr Binder, as we waited outside the head teacher's office. "What were you fighting over?"

I actually wasn't sure how things had escalated quite so quickly. When I punched Ali on the arm, he was so shocked he thumped me back – HARD. So I gave him a shove. I didn't mean to push him off his chair!

At least we got the chance to warn the robot not to use his video eyes when he came to break us up. So you could say that the plan worked perfectly! Except for the part where we got sent to the head teacher.

"What if she rings my mum?" said Ali. **"OR TELLS MY AUNTIE?"**

"The important thing is we stopped Robin from letting everyone know he's a robot!" I told him. "That would have been much worse than any punishment we'll get."

"You don't know my auntie!" Ali muttered, as the door opened and Ms Sternwood beckoned us inside.

The head teacher gave us a lecture about

how "violence is never the answer" and that we should try to "talk through our problems". Then she made us shake hands and that was it.

"Told you there was nothing to worry about," I said, as we walked back to the classroom. "Sorry I pushed you off your chair!"

"Desperate times!" Ali grinned. "Though if it happens again, let's try something less painful."

"Agreed!" I said, rubbing my arm.

After lunch we were supposed to do PE, but instead of making us run around the field in the freezing cold, Robin announced that we were going to learn the dance routine from the Carly-G video.

"Dancing's not proper PE!" said Brett.

"Dance is an excellent form of exercise," said Robin. "It improves fitness, co-ordination *and* strength."

He told us that Carly-G's routine had been inspired by a traditional Māori dance. Watching Robin attempt to demonstrate with his robotic movements was so funny, I even forgot to worry for a while.

When Ms Sternwood came in to see what all the laughing was about, we gave her a demonstration, calling out the moves in *te reo*, the language spoken by the Māori people.

"I'm impressed," she said, smiling at Robin. "PE, geography *and* language-learning – very cross-curriculum."

And then the bell rang, which meant that somehow we'd made it through a whole day with Robin as our teacher. Now we could get him home, call Grandma, and put everything back to how it was supposed to be.

SAVING THE DAY

Normally at the end of school Robin would be waiting with Digby at the gate to walk us home. We had no idea what Mr Mitchell would do.

Jess went to collect the dog from Mr Binder while I hung around until I was the only one left in the classroom.

"School is finished for the day, Student Jake," said Robin. "It is time to go home."

"Don't you need to go home too?"

"I am a teacher," he said. "School is my home."

"No, school is where you work," I told him.

"Teachers have homes too. You live with me and Jess."

The robot shook his head. "Your information is incorrect. I do not live with *MeandJess*. My place is in the classroom."

I was so frustrated I wanted to shake him!

Maybe that was it! Maybe another bang on the head would help?

My eyes drifted towards the giant dictionary on the shelf behind Mrs Badoe's desk…

"Jake? What are you doing with that dictionary?"

I didn't hear Ms Sternwood come in.

"Um … just looking up a word, miss!" I lowered the book.

"Isn't it time you went home?"

"Yes, miss."

Jess and Digby were waiting for me at the gate. I told my sister what Robin had said.

"And your solution was to hit him over the head with a dictionary?!"

"I didn't actually DO IT! Anyway, it might have worked – you don't know!"

My sister rolled her eyes. "If you hadn't left him alone in the staffroom, none of this would have happened!"

"How was I to know he'd reset and think he was a teacher?"

"Well, you can tell Mum," said Jess.

"He thinks he's a WHAT?" Mum had just got back from a double shift at work. She was tired and struggling to understand how our robot babysitter was now our robot teacher.

"We need to phone Grandma," I said.

"She'll know what to do."

"Grandma's at Granny Anderson's," said Mum.

I'd forgotten Grandma had gone to visit *her* mum in Scotland for Hogmanay. "I'll call her."

"He thinks he's a WHAT?" said Grandma.

I sighed and went through it all again.

"The accident must have messed up his circuits," said Grandma, her voice sounding far away. "The version of his operating system where he's your babysitter must have got corrupted."

"But why does he think he's a teacher?"

"When you reset him it's like a fresh start," she said. "If the first thing somebody told him was that he was a teacher, he'd take that as his primary function and automatically boot up the relevant software."

"Does he even know he's a ROBOT?"

"Oh, yes!" said Grandma. "That's in his core programming."

"He's not very good at keeping it a secret."

Grandma chuckled. "You have to remember that robots are pure logic, Jake. They find it difficult to act human because much of our behaviour is so illogical."

"So how do we get *our* Robin back?"

The line crackled. "I'll have a look at him when I get home," she said.

"When's that going to be?"

"Not for a while, I'm afraid. Granny Anderson has some…" The connection went all fuzzy. I heard the word "turnip" then something that sounded like "deranged badger" then "…we can't expect her to be doing that on her own at ninety-four!"

"But what about Robin?"

"Sorry, Jake! I have to scoot! Granny Anderson just…" The next bit was swallowed by static and then the line went dead.

"Mum just told Mr Burton that Robin won't be able to work for him because he's got another job," said Jess, standing in the doorway to my bedroom. "You should have seen his face!" My sister hadn't looked this happy since Christmas morning.

With everything else that had happened, I'd forgotten all about our neighbour.

"So Robin becoming Mr Mitchell might actually be a good thing!" I said.

My sister's expression returned to its usual scowl.

"Think about it," I told her. "We've been saved from the torture of Ms Sternwood and 'Iggy Piggy', and now Robin won't have to go and work for Mr Burton!"

"I suppose…" said Jess.

"And if Robin becoming Mr Mitchell is MY fault like you said it was – that means I actually saved the day!"

THE CARDBOARD
LADY

"You think Robin stayed in the classroom all
night?" said Jess.

Mum had dropped us at school on her way
to work. It meant we were extra early, but that
gave us a chance to check on Robin before
anyone else arrived. Officially we weren't
allowed in school yet, so we had to make sure
nobody saw us.

The lights were on in most of the
classrooms and we could see teachers inside.
Our room was ominously dark.

"What if he's gone?" said Jess.

"Where would he go? You should have heard him last night – *My place is in the classroom!*" I put on a robotic voice and grinned, but my sister just scowled and opened the door.

It felt strange creeping into our classroom in the dark.

Jess pulled out a torch and shone the beam around the room. "He's not here!"

"Maybe he's gone to the staffroom for a coffee?"

"He's A ROBOT, dummy! They don't drink coffee!"

"So wh—"

"SHUSH!"

For a moment

I thought the caretaker was coming to tell us off, but the sound hadn't come from outside.

I walked over to the tiny storeroom where Mrs Badoe kept new exercise books and boxes of pencils, and pulled open the door.

Robin was standing in the tiny space between the shelves, plugged into the wall – recharging.

"WHAT is he WEARING?"

"That's what teachers used to wear in Victorian times!" said Jess. "I bet he looked up *teacher* on the internet and found a picture of someone dressed like that!"

"Good job we found him before anyone else!" I said.

The robot's eyes snapped open at the sound of our voices. "Student Jake, Student Jess," he said. "Class does not start for thirty-two minutes and seventeen seconds."

"That should give you time to change then," said Jess. "Teachers don't dress like that these days!"

"Oh!" Robin sounded disappointed. "Will I not be needing this then, either?" He pulled an evil-looking cane from inside his robes.

"NO!" we said together.

Then we heard the sound of footsteps approaching.

"We need to go," said Jess. "Get those things off before anyone sees you."

"And remember," I said, "try not to do anything too ... robot-ish today. If anyone finds out what you are, it would be REALLY BAD!"

"May I ask how you discovered I am not human?" said Robin.

"Because our grandma made you! Like I told you yesterday, you're—"

But there was no time to explain. Jess was already dragging me back outside.

I missed Robin, but Mr Mitchell *was* a good teacher. Normally I hate maths, but that morning the robot had turned learning equations into a code-breaking game that was so much fun even Brett didn't complain.

So when Ms Sternwood knocked on our classroom door and I saw that she wasn't alone, for a horrible moment I thought the *real* Mr Mitchell had arrived. Then I realized it wasn't even a real person.

"Can anyone tell me who this is?" The head teacher pointed to the life-sized cardboard cutout she was holding.

Olivia's hand shot into the air. "That's Fleur

Pickles, miss — from the telly!"

"Very good, Olivia. Ms Pickles and I are here to tell you about a very exciting competition." She indicated the large speech balloon coming from Fleur Pickles' mouth.

ENTER THE NATIONWIDE SCHOOLS' SCIENCE PROJECT, WIN PRIZES AND MONEY FOR YOUR SCHOOL. CREATE AN INVENTION TO HELP ME MAKE TOMORROW A REALITY TODAY!

"I'd like Year Six to enter," said Ms Sternwood.

"Impossible!" said Robin.

The head teacher almost dropped Fleur Pickles in surprise. "I beg your pardon?"

"We cannot make tomorrow TODAY!" said Robin. "If tomorrow was today, it would be today, and today would be yesterday! The cardboard lady has set an impossible task."

She stared at him.

"He's done it now!" whispered Ali. "That was SO robot!"

Ms Sternwood forced a smile. "Mr Mitchell reminds us how important it is to use language accurately. However, I think we understand what Ms Pickles *means* when she asks us to make tomorrow a reality today."

Sanjit raised his hand. "Does she want us to build a time machine, miss?"

Ms Sternwood looked like she wished *she* had a time machine to take her back to the moment before she'd walked into our classroom. But with no such device to hand, she battled on. "As I was saying … the schools with the best ideas will be invited to present their inventions at the Science EXPO in Birmingham. Wouldn't that be fun?"

The head teacher wasn't exactly knocked over by a wave of enthusiasm.

"Marston Manor are going to enter," she said, her eyes narrowing. "I believe they're building a rocket! But we don't want *them* to win, do we?"

Marston Manor School was in the leafy outskirts of town. The fact that Ms Sternwood's sister was head teacher there added extra spice to the rivalry.

"But Marston Manor always beat us at everything!" said Sanjit.

"Maybe it's time we did something about that," said Ms Sternwood, a growl creeping into her voice. "We need an invention that is so brilliant it will DESTROY Marston Manor once and for all! *Then* we'll see who's laughing!"

For a moment the head teacher seemed lost in her daydream of revenge, then she noticed the startled faces staring at her and gave an embarrassed smile. "Anyhow, I'll leave it with you. I'm sure that with Mr Mitchell's help you'll come up with something wonderful!"

Then she tucked Fleur Pickles under her arm and marched out of the room.

Grandma had told me that whoever gave Robin his first command after rebooting would become his primary operator. Ms Sternwood was that person and now she'd given the robot a new instruction – to win the science project competition and destroy her sister and the kids at Marston Manor in the process. It quickly became clear that Robin was determined to complete his mission. There was only one problem … US!

It was all very well having a super computer for a brain, but there was still the human factor to consider — or to put it another way, thirty Year Six kids guaranteed to mess things up.

Robin had asked the class to suggest ideas for our science project and written them on the whiteboard. I looked at the results:

TIME MACHINE. (No prizes for guessing whose idea that was!)

INVISIBILITY CLOAK.

A WAY TO TURN CHOCOLATE COINS INTO REAL MONEY.

JET PACK. (I'm pretty sure that one already exists.)

HOVER BOARD.

A ROBOT TO DO YOUR HOMEWORK FOR YOU. (That one made me nervous — had someone guessed the truth?)

TELEPORTATION DEVICE.

The few reasonable ideas would have required a laboratory of trained scientists, billions of pounds of funding and years of research. The rest were plain fantasy.

The robot stroked his beard and frowned. I guessed he was finally realizing the size of the task ahead. "To solve a problem, we begin by analyzing the available resources. You!" He pointed at us. "We need to discover what skill each of you has. We then combine those skills in the best way to achieve our desired result."

"But what if we haven't got any skills?" said Sanjit.

"Yeah!" said Brett. "What if we're just rubbish? You can't make a science project out of rubbish!"

"Maybe we can!" I said. I'd just remembered something I'd seen on TV over Christmas and it had given me an idea. "What if we took rubbish … and turned it into something else?"

Olivia snorted, but Robin was smiling. "Your idea has potential, Student Jake," he said.

Then Clara started signing.

Robin looked at her and nodded. "Clara says that organic matter produces methane gas that can be used as a fuel."

"Ms Sternwood said Marston Manor are building a rocket," said Olivia. "We're not going to beat that with smelly gas!"

"We could make a gas-powered rocket," said Sanjit.

"Yeah! We could send Ham into space!" said Ali. "He could be the first Ham on the moon!"

"That is too dangerous!" said Ivana.

"What about a car?" said Jess. "We could make an Eco Hamster Car, powered by gas made from rubbish. We might get extra points for being ecological!"

Robin stroked his beard for a moment then nodded. "I believe that this idea has a sixty-eight per cent chance of winning the competition."

When we heard that, even Brett seemed vaguely interested.

THE SKILLS HAT

When we came back after break there was a
strange contraption at the front of the classroom.

"What is THAT?" said Ali.

"Aha!" said Robin, emerging from the
cupboard in a white lab coat. "I have built a
device to extract data from each student to
identify their special skills."

"*Extract?*" said Ali. "Won't that be painful?"

"Not at all," said the robot, fastening Ali
into the chair. "I ran a test on the furry rodent
during break. You have nothing to fear."

"You tested it on HAM?" Ivana looked horrified.

"What skills does *he* have?" asked Brett, peering into the hamster cage.

"The rodent is very good at escaping," said Robin. "He often ventures out at night to eat the Play-Doh."

"So that's why his poo is all those funny colours," said Sanjit.

Ali didn't look at all reassured as the robot lowered the modified colander on to his head. There were thick wires running from Mrs Badoe's computer attached to it.

"What if it does something funny to my brain?" asked Ali.

"It'll have to find it first," said Jess.

"You may feel a slight tingle," said Robin, tapping the keyboard.

"A slight wha— Oooh!" Ali grinned and went all cross-eyed.

A minute later it was over.

"So what's Ali good at, sir?" said Sanjit.

The robot peered at the screen. "Student Ali is hard-working and good at following instructions. His special skills include computers and magic tricks."

Ali blushed. "Um … I don't actually *do* magic any more. That was, like, years ago!"

But nobody was listening, they were too busy arguing over who should go next.

Robin gave everyone in the class a job based on the data he'd collected with the Skills Hat.

Jess loves telling people what to do, so she was made Production Manager. Ali's computer skills were assigned to record and catalogue the project. Clara, who is brilliant at chemistry, was in charge of turning the rubbish into fuel, while Olivia's sense of style was put to use designing a flashy paint job for the Hamster Dragster.

Ivana makes her own clothes and loves cars, so she was in the group building the vehicle. I wanted to be in that team too, but Jess pointed out how clumsy I am. Instead, the robot made me Roving Problem Solver because the Hat said I was good at coming up with solutions to problems. It would be my job to offer advice to any team that ran into difficulty – but I had strict instructions not to touch anything! Sanjit spent a long time in the chair and was eventually made Crew Manager, which meant it was his job to look after our hamster test pilot.

Finally, Robin told Brett that the data had revealed him as the strongest member of the class and that this strength "would be a great asset" to the team. He was put in charge of waste collection and preparation. Brett shrugged like he wasn't bothered, but we all saw him smile.

We spent the whole afternoon working on our science project. When we got home there was a note from Mum reminding me to put out the recycling. I meant to do it straight away but I got distracted playing with Digby. By the time I remembered, it was dark and creepy outside, so when Mr Burton's head suddenly appeared above the fence, I jumped and dropped half the stuff.

"I wonder," said the old man, "what Ms Sternwood and the Class Six parents would think if they knew their children were being taught by an IMPOSTOR!"

I groaned, but I'd known all along it would only be a matter of time before Olivia or Brett blabbed to their grandad!

"Sorry … I don't know what you mean!"

"Don't play dumb with me, boy! I know it's your robot masquerading as a teacher! What do you think would happen if people were to find out, eh?" His face split into a mean smile.

I imagined the front page of the local newspaper.

Hardacre Herald

IS MY TEACHER A ROBOT?

A

I couldn't think of an excuse, so I tried the truth. "Robin didn't mean to lie to anyone!" I said. "He had an accident. It messed up his memory. He believes he really is our teacher!"

For a moment I saw a flicker of doubt, then Mr Burton's face hardened. "All the more reason to put a stop to it! Parents have a right to know their children are being taught by an unqualified person — especially when it's a ROBOT!"

Before I could think of anything else to say, our neighbour melted back into the darkness, leaving me with an armful of recycling and a horrible feeling that things had just taken a huge turn for the worse.

EXPECTING
THE WORST

I expected to find reporters at the school gate next morning and Robin being led away by men in black suits and sunglasses, but nothing happened. I guessed Mr Burton hadn't told anybody yet. But he would.

"We have to do something!" said Ivana.

We all agreed on that. The problem was nobody could think WHAT to do.

"If Brett's grandad's doing this because he wants the robot to go and work for him," said Ali, "maybe we could persuade Robin to go round there?"

"And threaten him?" said Jess, her eyes
lighting up. "I like your thinking! Have we still got
that leaf-blower?"

"I *meant* we get Robin to go and work for
Mr Burton – in the evenings."

"No way!"

"I know you don't want him to, Jake, but
which is worse? Robin being Mr Burton's slave
for a few weeks, or the whole world finding
out that he's a you-know-what?"

It wasn't the worst idea in the world. And,
more importantly, it was all we had.

We decided to stay behind at break so we
could talk to Robin, but the second the bell
went, the robot disappeared outside with Brett
and his Rubbish Collection Crew.

We followed them to the side of the school
where the recycling bins were.

"Mr Mitchell? Can we talk to you for a

minute?" I glanced across to where Brett and his gang were emptying kitchen scraps into a wheelbarrow, hoping they wouldn't be able to hear us.

"You require education?" asked Robin, climbing into a metal bin filled with cardboard boxes.

I tried to explain about Mr Burton, but it was hard when all I could see were the robot's legs sticking out.

"Your sixty seconds have elapsed," he said, emerging with a stack of soggy boxes.

"What?"

"You asked to talk for a minute."

"Did you not hear what I said? Mr Burton is going to tell everyone that you're a robot!"

"I do not know Mr Burton."

"Actually, you do – you've just forgotten," said Jess. She tried to explain it all again.

"We were thinking," said Ali, "if you went round there after school … and helped him … then maybe he won't tell anyone."

"And you'll be able to stay as our teacher," said Ivana.

We'd hoped Robin would be impressed by our logic, but instead he got angry. "I'm a teacher, not a repair-bot! I have important work to do. We must destroy Marston Manor and make tomorrow a reality today! If you are not here to help, please go away!" Then he dived head first back into the bin.

Every morning for the rest of that week and the next, I arrived at school expecting the worst, but it didn't happen.

"Maybe Brett persuaded him not to say anything?" said Ali at lunchtime on Friday.

"Brett does seem to like Mr Mitchell," I said. "I don't think he's beaten anyone up yet this week."

"He's too busy menacing kids for their leftovers," said Ali.

We watched as Brett worked his way across the dinner hall collecting food scraps for the science project. A lot of people were so scared of him, they gave up the contents of their lunch boxes whether they'd finished or not!

"You'd better eat that quick!" said Ali,

nodding at my sandwich. "He's coming over!"

But it wasn't my lunch Brett wanted.

"I need to talk to you," he said, glaring at the kids next to us until they moved to a different table. "My grandad's got a plan to get Mr Mitchell the sack!"

For a moment I thought Brett had come to gloat, but then I saw the worry in his eyes. "He wanted me to help, but I said no. So Olivia said she'd do it instead. Grandad promised he'd get her tickets to see Carly-G if she helped."

"What's she going to do?" said Ali.

"They wouldn't tell me." Brett frowned. "But it's something to do with the Gunk Gas." That was the name we'd given our eco-fuel. We were due to be testing it that afternoon.

"Why are you telling us this?" I asked him.

Brett shrugged. "I like Mr Mitchell. He lets me do stuff." Then he snatched my sandwich and walked away.

"Do you believe him?" said Ali.

"I don't know, but we can't risk it. We need to warn Robin!"

A STINKY TRICK

When we got to the classroom we found that everyone had come back early to help set up for the test run. It was impossible to get Robin alone so we could warn him.

"We'll just have to watch Olivia ourselves," I said. "And keep an eye on Brett – just in case."

Ali went to *help* Brett who was at the back of the classroom mashing the lunch scraps he'd collected to feed into the Gunk Chamber.

Creating the gas to power the Hamster Dragster was a three-stage process.

First we collected the rubbish – everything from compostable cardboard to food waste. Once Brett and his team of Mashers had crushed and torn it into small pieces, the mush was loaded into the Gunk Chamber to be "cooked".

Heat turned the rubbish into a sticky, stinky, greenish gunk – hence the name. This mixture was then siphoned into glass bottles and a large balloon was attached to the top. (This had to be done quickly because Gunk did

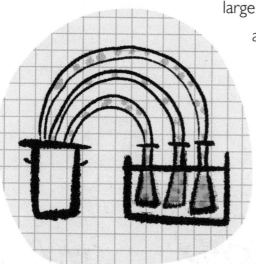

NOT smell good.)
The Gunk produced
a gas called
methane, which
over the course of
a few days filled the
balloons.

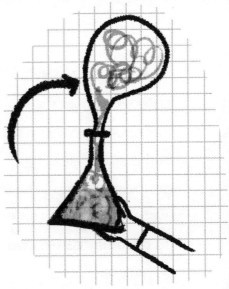

Finally, when the
balloons were inflated, they
could be attached to the Hamster Dragster
and the Gunk Gas would be released into the
engine to drive the car. Previous tests had shown
that we needed six balloons to provide enough
power, especially with a heavy hamster on board!

I was trying to follow Olivia without being too obvious. She hovered next to Ivana as final adjustments were made to the Hamster Dragster then stood behind Robin while he connected the six Gunk Gas balloons to the engine, but I didn't see her actually DO anything.

Robin started the final checks.

"Dragster team?"

"Ready!" said Ivana.

"Track marshals?"

"Ready!" said Jess.

"Fire and rescue?"

"Ready!" said Sanjit, clutching a bucket of sand.

Robin nodded to me.

I turned to face the mobile phone that Ali was using to video the test run. "This is Northfield Park Primary, Year Six," I said, into the camera. "Hamster Dragster powered by Gunk Gas™. Test run number nine." Then I stepped out of the shot so Ali could focus on the action.

"All crew, clear the area," said Robin.

There were safety shields for us to stand behind while Robin fired up the Dragster, but nothing to protect him. What if Mr Burton planned to do more than get Robin sacked? What if he wanted to hurt him?

"Starting ignition sequence," said Robin.

Suddenly, I had a horrible thought – what if Olivia had already sabotaged the Gunk Gas?

"Fuel valve open."

She could have done it this morning before Brett warned us.

"Electric starter, in three…"

She could have sneaked into the classroom during break or lunchtime!

"Two!"

"WAIT!" I shouted.

At least, that's what I meant to say. But my throat seized up in panic and all that came out was a strangled squeak.

"One!" said Robin – and pressed the starter.

The Hamster Dragster tore across the tables in a blur of glitter and everyone cheered.

Ali swung the camera back to me. Unfortunately, the switch from panic to relief had left me speechless. I stared into the camera, my mouth gaping like a fish.

Jess pushed me aside and delivered the prepared line about a successful test run.

"That's a wrap!" said Ali, then turned to me. "What was that all about? You

made a really weird noise."

"I thought…" I shook my head. "Nothing happened."

"You think Brett was winding us up?"

We looked over to where Brett was fastening the lid on the Gunk Chamber. He pressed a button and an orange light came on to show the chamber was heating up. Next to it was a stack of empty lunch boxes. Brett started handing them back to their owners. There was a sparkly silver container with a picture of Carly-G on the lid that had to belong to Olivia. Sure enough, Brett dropped it on to his cousin's table. Olivia picked up the box and looked inside, then smiled to herself.

It felt like somebody had dropped an ice cube down my back.

The light on the Gunk Chamber flickered from orange to red. The Gunk had started to cook.

"NO!"

"What?" said Ali.

"She tricked us!" I said.

"What are you on about?"

There was no time to explain. I called out to Brett, but he didn't hear. Then Olivia looked right at me and smiled. It was a nasty, triumphant *HA!* kind of smile.

Which is when I knew for certain.

I had to get to the Gunk Chamber and switch it off before whatever had been in Olivia's lunch box did what Mr Burton wanted.

I was halfway across the room when the smell hit me in the back of the throat. It was so bad I threw up my lunch before I could stop myself.

All around me kids were being sick. Then I saw the green smoke curling out from under the lid of the Gunk Chamber like some strange Halloween fog.

"EVERYBODY, OUT!" shouted Robin.

It was a messy exit – kids falling over each other, slipping in what was on the floor. In all the confusion nobody but me saw Olivia take off the nose peg. By the time we got outside, she was coughing and spluttering like everyone else – going on about how it was the Gunk that had made us sick.

Unfortunately, Ms Sternwood and most of the parents blamed the Gunk too – or more precisely, they blamed Mr Mitchell.

CHAPTER 11

MISSION TERMINATED

Robin might have survived if the substitute teacher agency hadn't phoned Ms Sternwood that afternoon to ask if she still needed staff. Apparently, they were very surprised to hear that *Mr Mitchell* had been at the school since the start of term, when according to their records he was teaching in Bromsgrove.

Robin tried to convince Ms Sternwood that he *was* the real Mr Mitchell – which of course he truly believed – but a gang of adults led by Mr Burton said they didn't want him teaching their children, and that was that.

In the end it was quite easy to persuade Robin to come home with us. The moment Ms Sternwood sacked him, all her previous instructions were terminated. The robot still believed he was Mr Mitchell, but now he was a teacher with no school, no students to educate, and nowhere else to go.

"Maybe when he sees the house he'll remember who he really is," said Jess.

When Digby saw the robot, I thought he was going to take off, his tail was wagging so fast. But Robin still didn't recognize the dog or the house.

"Perhaps it'll take a while," said Mum.

The robot wandered from room to room then sat down in the kitchen and plugged himself in to recharge. Digby took up his old position at Robin's feet, but the robot barely noticed him.

I called Grandma to find out when she was coming home, but the line was awful. I heard something about "a wet kipper" and possibly "kung fu"… Basically she wasn't coming back any time soon.

"What's wrong with Robin?" said Dad, when he got home. "He looks kind of … depressed."

We all looked at Robin, the mortar board crooked on his head, dejectedly flexing his cane.

"Maybe it's because robots are designed

93

to do things," I said. "He probably feels useless without a mission."

"He needs a job," said Dad.

"I doubt another school will employ him after what happened," said Mum.

"Not in a school." Dad's eyes flicked towards next door. "I was thinking…"

"No way!" My shout was so loud it woke the dog. "Mr Burton got him sacked!"

"You know what's odd?" said Mum. "For all his meddling, Mr Burton hasn't told anyone that Robin is a ROBOT – just that he isn't a qualified teacher."

"We're supposed to be grateful, are we?" I growled.

She shrugged. "Imagine if word had got out. It would be all over the newspapers by now. Then where would we be?"

"Your mum's right," said Dad. "We should be glad that Robin's home with his secret intact.

When Grandma gets back she'll fix him and we'll get our old Robin again. In the meantime we might as well let the robot go and help Mr Burton. It'll give him a purpose *and* get the old man off our back!"

I tried to tell myself that they were right, but I couldn't be happy about it.

We arrived at school on Monday and found Ms Sternwood and her guitar back in our classroom.

"Right!" she said. "Who remembers the 'Fractions Song'?"

I groaned. But that was just the start.

On Wednesday she handed out recorders and tried to teach us 'Baby Baby Baby', by Carly-G. Not even Olivia enjoyed that.

By the time Friday arrived I was seriously considering stealing Ms Sternwood's guitar…

Then, incredibly, something good happened.

We were in the middle of a lesson on rivers when Mr Binder came in looking excited.

"Guess whose science project made it through to the final?" he said, handing a large envelope to the head teacher.

"We didn't!"

"Oh, yes, you did!"

Ms Sternwood glanced towards the Gunk-coloured stain on the back wall. After the incident, our science project had been cancelled by parental demand.

"Marston Manor have been picked for the final too," said Mr Binder, giving a thumbs down. Some of the class booed.

"Have they indeed!" Ms Sternwood narrowed her eyes. "We can't let them have it all their own way, can we? The school's reputation is at stake here!"

"But, miss?" Sanjit raised his hand. "I thought

we weren't allowed to make any more Gunk Gas?"

Ms Sternwood looked at him, then she walked over and closed the door.

"Well," she said, "we'll have to see about that, won't we?"

CHAPTER 12

SCIENCE CLUB

"The first rule of Science Club," said Ms Sternwood, "is that you don't talk about Science Club! This has to be our secret."

Officially we weren't allowed to work on our science project any more — at least not during school hours — which was why Ms Sternwood had started an after-school club.

The final at the Science EXPO in Birmingham was only three weeks away and the head teacher had already booked a coach. All we had to do now was get Gunk Gas production running again. But there was a problem – the Gunk Chamber had been damaged in the accident and nobody knew how to fix it.

While Ali looked online, Jess, Clara and Ms Sternwood tried to decipher Robin's original plans, and Brett went outside to collect rubbish. An hour later Brett was back, happily mashing up ingredients to make Gunk – but the chamber wasn't ready.

"We need Mr Mitchell," said Ali. "He's the only one who can fix this."

Ms Sternwood frowned. "That man lied to me!"

"It looks like Marston Manor are going to beat us again then," said Jess, to nobody in particular.

The head teacher flinched. "I suppose it wouldn't hurt to ask Mr Mitchell back in an advisory role," she said. "He wouldn't actually be *teaching*…"

We couldn't wait to get home and give Robin the good news. He'd been working at Mr Burton's all day and was covered in dust and dirt. When the robot read the note from Ms Sternwood, he was so happy he did the dance from the Carly-G video all round the kitchen!

"So what's Mr Burton got you doing next door?" I asked, when Robin finally sat down.

"I'm afraid I'm not at liberty to say," said the robot. "Mr Burton has informed me that our work is strictly confidential."

I snorted. "What's confidential about fixing a house?"

Robin didn't answer.

"Burton's up to something," I told Jess, but she just laughed.

"You always think *somebody's* up to *something*!"

"That's because they usually ARE!" I said, but nobody was listening.

You'd have thought Carly-G had arrived, from the reception Robin received at Science Club the following week. With his mission reinstated, the robot happily set to work fixing the Gunk

Chamber with Clara and Ivana. I noticed Ms Sternwood was keeping a close eye on things, so we had to keep reminding him not to act too much like a robot.

Robin's attempts to appear more human involved him dropping his screwdriver all the time and singing while he worked. Unfortunately, Ms Sternwood knew the song and joined in. It was a painful couple of hours, but by the time the head teacher locked up for the night, Brett had set the first new batch of Gunk cooking.

For the next two weeks life settled into a pattern. Robin still believed he was Mr Mitchell but agreed to walk us to school like he used to. Then he'd go next door and help Mr Burton. At the end of the day, the robot would be back to join us for Science Club where preparations for the final were going well. At least, they had been…

"Let me do it!" Ali took the half-empty gas balloon from Sanjit and crouched over the dragster. "All you've got to do is slide that on there and then … oh!"

The gas made a loud fart sound as it escaped from the balloon.

Nobody laughed. This was a serious problem.

"We can't get the balloons attached," I told Ms Sternwood. "If you're not quick enough, all the gas escapes!"

"Mr Mitchell usually does it," said Ali. "We're all too slow."

"Where *is* Mr Mitchell?"

"I don't know. He said he'd be here." I was worried. Robin is ultra reliable. Something must have happened to stop him from coming.

Ms Sternwood frowned. "How much gas do we have we left?"

"Two balloons here, plus the six for the presentation at the EXPO tomorrow," said Jess.

"We can't risk wasting any more," said the head teacher. "We'll just have to hope everything runs smoothly at the final. Mr Mitchell can definitely come with us?" The question was directed at me and Jess.

We nodded.

"We'll be fine then!" Ms Sternwood forced a smile. "Why don't we call it a night? We've got an early start tomorrow."

We ran all the way home, but when we got there the house was empty – except for Digby.

"Where's he gone, boy?"

The dog ran to the front door. When I

opened it he squirmed through the fence and started barking at Mr Burton's garage.

"I bet the old man's got him working in there and wouldn't let him leave," I said, as we walked over.

"You're trespassing!" said Mr Burton, opening the door a crack. He didn't notice Digby squeeze inside.

"Where's Robin?" said Jess. "He was supposed to meet us at school."

"How am I supposed to know?"

Then the dog started barking.

The old man turned. "What's that mutt doing in my workshop?"

Digby was pawing at a large cardboard box on the floor.

"He's found something," said Jess, pushing past the old man.

"How dare y—" Whatever Mr Burton had planned to say was drowned out by my sister's scream.

She jumped back from the box, her eyes wide in horror. **"WHAT HAVE YOU DONE?"**

I ran over and looked inside.

Robin's head was lying among a mess of metal, circuit boards and wire.

"It malfunctioned again," said Mr Burton. "I took it apart to try to fix it, but the thing's faulty – barely fit for scrap!"

I stared at him, too shocked to speak.

That's when I noticed the object standing in the centre of the garage. It was mostly hidden under a tarpaulin, but there was something oddly

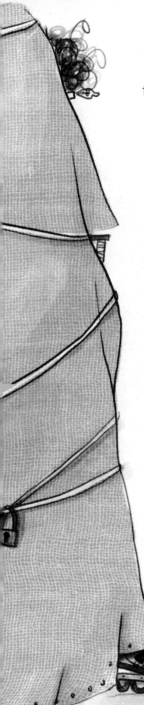

familiar about it…

I sprang across and pulled off the cover.

My sister gasped.

Suddenly, it ALL made sense. Now we knew why Mr Burton had wanted Robin so badly.

"YOU BUILT A ROBOT!"

Mr Burton tried to re-cover his creation, then shrugged. "I don't suppose it matters. When I go on *Buy It or Bin It?* tomorrow, the whole world will know!"

"You're going on TV?!"

A smug smile snaked across his face. "They're broadcasting a live show from the Science EXPO in Birmingham and I'm going to be on it."

"I suppose you're going to tell them that *you* invented that robot?" said Jess. "When all you did was dismantle Robin and steal Grandma's design!"

"It's your word against mine!" said Mr Burton, herding us out of his garage. "Who's going to believe you, when all that's left of *your* robot is a box of bits?" He thrust the box into my arms and slammed the door.

We walked home in stunned silence and put the box on the kitchen table.

"I KNEW he was up to something!" I said, but for once being able to say I TOLD YOU SO didn't bring any satisfaction at all.

"How could he do this?" Jess lifted Robin's head from the box and cradled it like a baby. Digby was totally confused. He sniffed the head and wagged his tail, then started looking around for the rest of the robot.

There was a hard lump in my throat and
for a moment I thought I might cry. But that
wouldn't help Robin. So I got angry instead.
"We have to rebuild him!" I said, dragging
the box towards me. "We just need to find
the parts and join them back together – like
LEGO!"

"With no instructions?" said Jess. She held up
a mysterious circuit board with wires dangling
from it. "Any idea where this bit goes?"

"I don't care, we have to try! I want Robin

back. If we do nothing it means HE'S won."

Then the doorbell rang.

"If that's Burton, I'm going to set the dog on him!" I growled.

But it wasn't the old man, it was Ivana with a sleeping bag under her arm. With all the drama we'd forgotten she was coming for a sleepover so she could walk with us to catch the coach in the morning.

Ivana gasped when she saw Robin in pieces on the table. Then she started moving the parts around … and gradually the jumble of random fragments began to resemble a robot again.

"It is like making clothes," she said. "You arrange the sections and then stitch them together. Only this is a bit more complicated."

"That's what I told Jake," said Jess.

"But we can do it!" There was a defiant edge to Ivana's voice. "Like Robin said – we can do anything if we use our skills and work together!"

Jess gave a doubtful nod.

"I'll call Ali," I said. "We're going to need all the help we can get!"

CHAPTER 13

WE CAN REBUILD HIM!

A storm was brewing outside and rain rattled the windows as we gathered around the robot lying in pieces on the kitchen table. My sister had Grandma on video chat from Scotland, so we could show her the parts and she could tell us which bits went where. Then me and Jess held things in place while Ivana did the technical stuff that required a steady hand and skilful fingers. Ali didn't want anything to do with *innards* and *body parts*, so he was busy on his laptop preparing the software we would need to get Robin working again.

When Mum got back from her shift at the pub it was gone midnight. She was dripping wet from the rain and not happy to discover that the kitchen had been turned into a robot operating theatre. I thought she might send us to bed, but instead she made a big stack of toast, then left us to it.

By the time Mum went upstairs, Robin was starting to look like a robot again. He had a body with arms and legs – well, one and a half legs anyway. The bottom of Robin's left leg was missing, as were his special wheeled shoes.

By 2 a.m. there were only a handful of parts left and it was time to reattach Robin's head.

"This bit might be tricky," said Grandma, her voice crackling as the storm wreaked havoc with the video link.

"I can do it," said Ivana. "Jake, you will need to hold the head very still while I solder the wires."

It felt weird holding Robin's lifeless head in my hands. It was heavy and my arms shook with the effort of holding it in position. I could smell the hot solder, hear it hissing under the heat of the soldering iron as Ivana joined the wires in a bead of liquid silver.

"Almost done," she said.

It was the thunder that made me jump.
A booming roar that sounded like the house
was falling down. The head slipped from my
grip … and Ivana screamed.

"I am fine!" Ivana managed to smile while Jess
bandaged her hand, but there was no way she'd
be doing any more robot surgery. Luckily, she'd
attached the last wire before I trapped her
fingers under Robin's head.

"There aren't many pieces left now,
Grandma," I said. "But we're not sure where this
goes." I held up a short metal bracket with a
spring at the end.

"Ah," said Grandma. "That's his shvridy-
ung-lack-mmm-kkkzzt." The storm was
getting worse and it was interfering with
the connection. "You need ggrkk-shtuk-um
quite important!"

"Sorry, Grandma," said Jess. "We didn't get that."

On screen Grandma was flickering. "Shkurg oom nash nash fellack," she said, then the picture froze.

"We've lost WiFi," said Ali. "It might come back, but we can't wait. We need to start him up. I still have to install the software and we've got to be at school to catch the coach in a few hours!"

"But Grandma just told us these leftover parts are important!" I said.

Jess shrugged. "Maybe when we get him going, Robin will be able to tell us where they go."

We connected the lead from Ali's laptop and gathered round. This was the moment of truth. The figure lying on the kitchen table *looked* like Robin, but could we really bring him back to life?

Thunder shook the windows as lightning

lit up the room.

"OK," said Ali. "Here goes. Start-up in ten, nine…"

Jess rolled her eyes and jammed a finger up Robin's nostril.

There was a click, followed by a whirr of machinery in the depths of Robin's chest.

"I'm getting a read-out," said Ali, his eyes on the screen. "Looking good so far."

We watched the silent form on the table, willing it to move.

Another rumbling boom overhead and a double flash threw jagged silhouettes across the figure on the table.

"Look!" said Jess. "His fingers are moving."

"He's ALIVE!" I said.

The robot blinked and slowly rolled his head to look at us. "Master Jake," he said. "Miss Jess!"

"It's ROBIN!" I said. "He's back!"

WHAT'S WRONG
WITH HIM?

"I can't believe we rebuilt him *and* got his memory back!" said Ali, yawning as we walked to school to catch the coach.

I smiled. We'd done well, but we hadn't *quite* managed to put Robin back together exactly as he had been before.

"Oh, my! What happened to you?" Ms Sternwood's face dropped when she saw the robot.

"Mr Mitchell broke his ankle, miss," said Jess. "That's why he missed Science Club yesterday."

We'd improvised a cast to cover Robin's missing half-leg. Luckily, we still had the crutches from when Dad injured his foot dancing at the Metal Mayhem festival. But it was the robot's satnav speech processor that was worrying me most.

"It's very nice to see you again," Robin told Ms Sternwood. "At the roundabout, take the second exit."

The head teacher blinked. "I beg your pardon?"

"Um … we were talking about the best way to get to Birmingham from here," I said. "Which way to go at the big roundabout."

"I'll help Mr Mitchell on to the coach, miss," said Jess. "We don't want to be late."

Ms Sternwood gave a doubtful nod. "At least you're here – that's the main thing."

We'd barely reached the end of the road before the head teacher got out her guitar to *entertain* us. As the 'Gunk Gas Song' – *it's wonderFUEL* – reached its fifth verse, Ali tapped me on the shoulder.

"I think we might have a problem," he said. "I've been talking to Robin and … the thing is … now Robin's back, he doesn't remember being Mr Mitchell!"

"Is that all?" I laughed. "You had me worried for a minute!"

Ali shook his head. "You don't understand. Robin doesn't remember ANYTHING."

"So?"

Ivana leaned across the aisle. "That means he won't know how the science project works!"

"Oh, NO!"

The Science EXPO was packed with people buzzing round the stands where exhibitors in lab coats were showing off their inventions. A stage had been set up in one corner with a giant 3D version of the famous *Buy It or Bin It?* logo suspended from the ceiling. Just looking at it made me nervous.

A lady with a headset directed us backstage – a large space separated into cubicles with heavy curtains. There were schoolkids everywhere. Jess scowled when she spotted the burgundy uniforms from Marston Manor.

While Brett unloaded the equipment, we propped Robin into a chair. "Just sit there and try to look like you know what you're doing," I told him.

"In one hundred metres turn right into Conrad Drive," said the robot.

Luckily, the Mr Mitchell version of Robin had already set up most of what we needed earlier in the week.

"Now we just have to connect the gas," said Jess.

Brett distracted Ms Sternwood while we showed Robin the Hamster Dragster and explained what he needed to do.

"What a clever idea," said Robin. "At the traffic lights, turn right."

Clara handed him a balloon filled with Gunk Gas, but as the robot tried to connect it, we heard the familiar farty escape of gas.

"Please make a U-turn and rejoin the route," said Robin, which is when I noticed his thumb had fallen off.

"So that's where that bracket should have gone!" whispered Ali.

"NOW WHAT DO WE DO?" I hissed.

"You can do it, Master Jake," said Robin. "Follow the route to your destination."

"ME? No way! I'm rubbish at stuff like that. Ivana's the one with the clever hands."

Ivana raised her bandaged hand and gave a sad wave.

"Don't look at me," said Sanjit. "I'm not getting blamed when it all goes wrong!"

Ali suddenly needed the toilet and Clara was nowhere to be seen.

"Give it to me," said Jess.

I held my breath as my sister positioned the balloon over the inlet pipe and carefully stretched the neck over the nozzle … then let go.

The balloon stayed inflated.

"How did you…?" I stared at my sister.

"I'm a genius," said Jess. "Keep up." Then she attached the other four balloons. The final one would have to be done as part of the demonstration – **IN FRONT OF THE JUDGES** – but Jess said she could do it.

"The students have all the roundabouts they need to perform the demonstration without turning left," Robin told Ms Sternwood.

"It's the pills the hospital gave him for the pain, miss," said Ali, shaking his head.

The head teacher agreed it would probably be best if Mr Mitchell didn't come on stage with us.

It was noisy backstage. You could hear people talking in the area next to ours. I gradually became aware of a familiar voice on the other side of the curtain.

"… the world's first fully functioning

humanoid robot," the voice was saying. "It's going to change the way we live forever."

Me and Jess exchanged a look, then pushed through a gap in the partition.

Mr Burton was showing off his robot to Fleur Pickles. I recognized her from the telly and the cardboard cutout at school, though she looked a lot less flat in real life. Olivia was there, too, trying to sneak a photo of herself standing next to Fleur without the woman realizing – which was quite easy because Fleur Pickles had just noticed my sister storming towards them like an angry Rottweiler.

"He's a liar and a THIEF!" shouted Jess, jabbing a finger at Mr Burton. "He stole the design from our grandma!" Then she grabbed a large spanner from a nearby table and lunged towards the old man's robot.

But before Jess could do any damage, a
large security guard grabbed the weapon and
dragged my sister away.

I was about to go after them when Ali appeared. "Jake! It's time."

"But Jess just…

She's…

WHO'S GOING TO ATTACH THE BALLOON?"

"You'll have to do it," said Ali, pushing me up the stairs and on to the stage.

TEAPOTS, ROBOTS AND FLYING HAMSTERS!

The ground felt wobbly under my feet as I stumbled on to the stage and joined my classmates behind the tables where our science project was laid out.

Brett stood proudly beside a pile of rotting food waste. Next to him, Clara waited to demonstrate the Gunk Chamber, before Ali transferred the Gunk into bottles and I revealed how we used balloons to capture the gas. Ivana had a microphone so she could explain as we demonstrated. Sanjit was at the end of the row with Ham, but there was a gap next to them, behind the table with the two balloons of Gunk Gas waiting to be attached to the Dragster. A gap where Jess should have been.

Ms Sternwood and Robin were watching from the audience. When the head teacher registered that Jess was missing, her eyes widened in horror. But before she could do anything, Fleur Pickles strode on to the platform.

"Ladies and gentlemen, girls and boys! Welcome to the final of this year's…"

My brain was too busy panicking to listen. Without Jess to connect the gas we were doomed!

Then Fleur Pickles said the name of our school and we were off.

I kept waiting for Jess to appear, but she didn't, and then Ivana was saying, "Next, we attach the Gunk Gas balloon to the Hamster Dragster."

There was a pause.

Suddenly everyone was looking at me.

"Jake!" hissed Ali. "You'll have to do it!"

ME? I couldn't even tie my shoelaces without getting into a mess!

I could see Ms Sternwood glaring at me to get on with it, so I picked up one of the two remaining gas balloons and Ivana repeated her line.

With five attached already, there was hardly any space to slide the neck of the balloon over the end of the pipe. But after a lot of fumbling I did it.

At least I thought I had.

The moment I let go, the balloon made a loud farting noise – amplified by Ivana's microphone. Ms Sternwood buried her face in her hands as the audience roared with laughter.

"Attaching the balloon is a difficult process," said Ivana, improvising.

My hands were shaking as I reached for the final balloon.

I glanced up and saw Robin watching. He raised a hand to give me a thumbs up, but of course his thumb was missing.

Jess hadn't believed that we'd be able to rebuild the robot, but there he was.

Admittedly, he wasn't in full working order, but it was a pretty good effort for four ten-year-olds in one night. If we'd just given up, Robin would still be a box of bits on the kitchen table.

If the robot had taught us anything, it was that everybody had *something* they were good at. And if everyone worked together you could actually make something really amazing with what appeared to be useless rubbish!

It had been *my* idea that started it all off. So maybe I could finish it too?

I took a deep breath, then eased the neck of the balloon over the nozzle … and let go.

I waited for the fart and the laughter.

But it didn't happen. I'd done it!

Ali grinned as he took the fully fuelled dragster to Sanjit so our reluctant test pilot could be coaxed into his seat.

"A battery provides the spark to ignite the fuel," read Ivana, then started to count down.

The audience joined in –

"THREE!"

"TWO!"

"ONE!"

The other presentations passed in a blur. Before we knew it, we were sitting in the audience with Jess, Robin and Ms Sternwood waiting to hear Fleur Pickles announce the winner. For a moment I actually believed it might be us.

It wasn't.

But it wasn't Marston Manor either. A tiny primary school in North Wales won with their Non-Melting Ice Cream, which was actually pretty impressive – plus we all got a free sample!

We were still in the hall when the special live episode of *Buy It or Bin It?* started.

When Mr Burton appeared with his robot the audience gasped. Jess started muttering that she would have knocked the thing's head off if the security guy hadn't interfered.

Meanwhile, up on stage Mr Burton was boasting how his invention was going to change the world, while the robot – who he called Roberta – picked up a silver tray and started to serve tea to the judges.

"Why does it have to be serving tea?" said Ivana. "Couldn't it do something cool?"

But the judges looked impressed. They were asking Mr Burton lots of questions and seemed to like the answers.

"If he wins…" Jess growled.

Robin's eyes were fixed on the other robot and I noticed his lips were moving. I leaned closer, expecting to hear more random directions, but this was complete gibberish.

"That sounds like computer code," said Ali. "Like he's reciting lines of programming…"

"You think he's talking to Roberta?" I said.

"It's possible. They are the same design—"

A shriek from the stage distracted us.

I looked up and saw Fleur Pickles hopping around, flapping at her jacket.

"It just spilled tea all down her!" said Jess, laughing.

Having emptied the teapot over Fleur Pickles, Mr Burton's robot was now throwing teacups at the other investors.

"Wait!" said Mr Burton, as they fled the stage. "It's just teething problems. I can fix it!"

Then Roberta the Robot hit him over the head with the tea tray.

"You have arrived at your destination," said Robin. Then he looked at me and winked.

A FAMILY AFFAIR

It was two weeks after the EXPO and everyone was excited because our old teacher Mrs Badoe had brought her new baby into school.

"The noise the tiny human makes is disproportionate to its size," said Robin, raising his voice over the howling. Ms Sternwood had invited him to come into school three afternoons a week to help out. She still called him Mr Mitchell, so the robot had to pretend.

"Maybe a song would soothe her?" said

Ms Sternwood, reaching for her guitar.

"The tiny human wants to sleep," said Robin. "She did not like being woken up to come here. And she does not like her hat because it is itchy."

Mrs Badoe stared at Robin. "How do you know my baby doesn't like her hat?"

"She told me," said Robin.

"Uh-oh!" Ali whispered. "Now he's done it."

Mrs Badoe's eyes boggled. "But she's a baby! She can't speak!"

"There are many ways to communicate that do not require speech," said Robin.

Ms Sternwood chuckled. "Mr Mitchell is a bit of a character! You get used to him after a while."

But our old teacher was still frowning. "Now I think about it … she always complains when I put that hat on her. I never knew it was because it itched."

Robin nodded. "She has a slight allergy to

wool. It's quite common and nothing to worry about. She also told me that—"

Olivia screamed.

Probably because Jess had just spilled a beaker of dirty painting water all over her.

"Sorry!" said Jess. "I tripped!"

She hadn't of course.

"Good diversion," whispered Ali, grinning at Jess.

It was nice to see Mrs Badoe, but I was glad when she left. The looks she was giving Robin were making me nervous, and there's only so many times you can throw water over someone – even Olivia.

"Wasn't that nice?" said Ms Sternwood. "It's a shame we didn't get to sing a song. How about we do one now?"

I couldn't believe my luck when the door opened again and Mr Binder announced we had ANOTHER special visitor.

Ms Sternwood almost fainted when Fleur Pickles swept into our classroom. She grabbed her hand and began pumping it up and down. "Look, children! Fleur Pickles! **FROM THE TELEVISION!**"

The celebrity entrepreneur smiled and gently prised her fingers free. "I came here today so I could tell you personally how impressed I was with your –" she paused and her assistant whispered in her ear – "Gunk Gas!" Fleur Pickles nodded. "If it had been up to me, you would have won!"

I'd never seen Ms Sternwood look so happy.

"Which is why I decided to award you a special prize." The assistant handed her a large gold trophy. "I also have a cheque, which I hope will enable you to continue the fantastic work you have started in your Science Club."

When she read the amount on the cheque Ms Sternwood had to sit down.

"I'll be keeping a close eye on your progress," said Fleur Pickles. "In fact, before I go I'd love to know what each of you is working on."

"NO!" hissed Jess. "What if she recognizes me from the EXPO?"

"Don't worry," said Ivana. "She won't."

But as Fleur Pickles reached us, she stopped and pointed a polished fingernail at my sister. "I know YOU! You're the girl with the spanner from the exhibition!" Then she laughed. "We should have let you clobber that robot. Ruined my best jacket, that thing!"

Jess nodded, too embarrassed to reply.

Then Fleur Pickles crouched down so she could speak without being overheard. "I seem to remember you saying something about your grandma inventing a robot."

"She tried," said Jess, "but she couldn't get it to work."

"Shame!" Fleur Pickles looked genuinely disappointed. "A humanoid robot – that really would be something!"

"Well done, Miss Jess," said Robin, when Fleur Pickles had gone. "Your grandma is anxious that my existence should be kept secret."

"About that," I said. "If you don't want people to guess that you're a robot, I'd try *not* having telepathic conversations with babies, then telling their mums everything they said!"

"Very well, Master Jake. I will add that advice to my database." The robot smiled. "You see, we are all teachers and we are all students. We have much to learn from each other. I believe there is much wisdom in this class."

I nodded.

Then Sanjit fell off his chair.

I guess some of us still have a lot to learn.

THE END (... or is it?)

Robin, Jake, Jess and the
gang will return for another
adventure very soon!

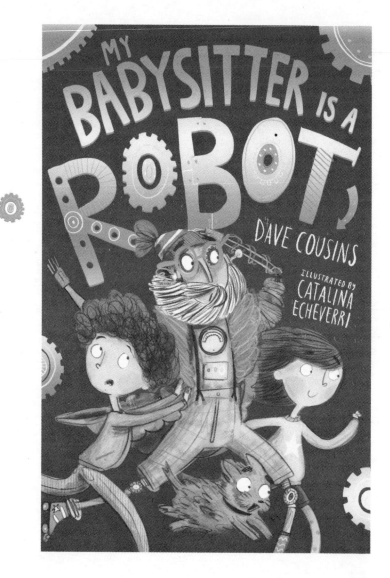

When Grandma creates a robot babysitter
for twins Jake and Jess, chaos ensues!

Robin is embarrassing, clumsy and, worst
of all, programmed to make them do their
homework. They're also pretty sure he thinks
their dog is a baby. The twins decide they have
to do something before everyone realizes that
Robin is a robot. But getting rid of their new
babysitter will mean putting aside their sibling
squabbles and working together, which might
be an even bigger challenge…

TURN THE PAGE TO SEE
HOW IT ALL BEGAN…

When I saw my sister waiting at the edge
of the playground, I knew straight away that
something was wrong.

Jess is my twin, which means we've been
stuck with each other our entire lives. I can't
even have a birthday without her getting in
the way! Of course Jess behaves like it's all MY
fault, as if I got born *deliberately* just to spoil
her fun. When we're at school, we try to have
as little to do with each other as possible,
which can be difficult when you're stuck in the
same class. So I can promise you that my sister
does NOT wait to walk home with me.

"Don't go out there!" Jess dragged me and
Ali back against the wall. "It's at the gate!" she
said. "WAITING FOR US!"

It took me a few seconds to work out that
she was talking about the robot. Jess was less

excited by the idea than me.

I peeked round the corner and spotted our new babysitter straight away. I'd like to say it was because our dog Digby was standing beside it, but that would be a lie. The robot was simply impossible to miss.

"Oh!" said Ali.

I wasn't sure *Oh!* quite covered it…

The thing is, as well as being an inventor, Grandma is a great believer in RECYCLING. She has three sheds, a garage and two bedrooms in her house full of stuff that "only needs a ——" (fill in the blank). Like the bicycle that "only needs a *wheel*", and the giant grandfather clock that "only needs an *hour hand*". It tells perfect time and chimes obediently every hour, except you can never be sure *which* hour.

The list goes on, but I won't. You get the idea.

Grandma hates waste, so the things she invents are always made from bits of other things that weren't meant to go together. Which probably explained why our new babysitter was wearing Grandma's old coat – the red one with the pink flowers and the furry collar.

"It looks like Father Christmas!" Jess groaned. "Look at that BEARD!"

"Grandma says that the beard hides the joins so you can't see it's not a real person!" I told her.

"Well, duh!" She frowned. "Hey! Are those my old Barbie skates?"

"And Dad's football hat."

"Um, I should get going," said Ali. "Auntie's waiting." He was embarrassed for me. We'd been expecting a cool robot like Bumblebee

… but the thing waiting at the gates looked more like Grandma with a beard!

I watched my friend run across the playground to where his aunt and a gaggle of little cousins were waiting. I was beginning to think that *he* was the lucky one.

Grandma must have programmed the robot to recognize us because as soon as we emerged from our hiding place it started waving.

"Miss Jess," said the robot. "Master Jake! How lovely to meet you." It sounded like Grandma putting on a deep voice, which is exactly what it was.

A ROBOT ATE MY GRANDMA

COMING SOON!

ABOUT THE AUTHOR

Abandoning childhood plans to be an astronaut –
or Batman – Dave Cousins went to art college in
Bradford, joined a band and was nearly famous.
His writing career began aged ten, drawing comics
and penning lyrics for an imaginary pop group.
Dave says that reading and writing stories helped him
along the bumpy path to growing-up, and hopes that his
books will play a similar role for today's readers.

When not scribbling stories and pictures,
Dave tours extensively. His events have been
described as "stand-up with books", or as
one reader put it: "well funny!" Dave has three
grown-up children and lives on a rock by the sea
in Wales, with his wife and a grumpy cat.

www.davecousins.net

ABOUT THE ILLUSTRATOR

Born in Bogotá, Colombia,
Catalina Echeverri lives in London with her
Northern Irish husband, Will, and their little daughter S.

Before settling in the UK Catalina spent time in Italy,
studying graphic design and eating pizza and ice cream
every day that she could. When she'd eaten it all, she
moved to Cambridge to study children's book illustration.
She has worked in children's publishing ever since, creating
books such as *Milo's Dog Says Moo*,
There's a Dinosaur in my Bathtub and *Lion and Mouse*.

Catalina is never without her sketchbook.
She particularly enjoys working on projects that
make a positive impact on people's lives.

www.cataverri.com